AUTHOR	HASTIE, E.	CLASS	F C

TITLE	Sherlock Holmes and the disappearing prince

D1354735

SHERLOCK HOLMES AND THE DISAPPEARING PRINCE

The Crown Prince of Japan disappears without trace from his Oxbridge college rooms. Relatives of an heiress meet, one by one, with suspicious and grisly deaths. The thief of confidential battleship plans must be identified and located before the documents are leaked to the German military. And what nefarious activity links a cabman charging extortionate fares with a musically-minded butler? Narrated with wry affection by the long-suffering Dr Watson, each problem in this collection of four short stories showcases Holmes' well-honed skills of ingenious analysis and consequential deduction to perfection . . .

EDMUND HASTIE

SHERLOCK HOLMES AND THE DISAPPEARING PRINCE
and Other Stories

Complete and Unabridged

LINFORD
Leicester

First published in Great Britain

First Linford Edition
published 2008

British Library CIP Data

Hastie, Edmund
  Sherlock Holmes and the disappearing
  prince.—Large print ed.—
  Linford mystery library
  1. Holmes, Sherlock (Fictitious character)—
  Fiction 2. Watson, John H. (Fictitious character)—
  Fiction 3. Detective and mystery stories, English
  4. Large type books
  I. Title
  823.9′2 [F]

  ISBN 978–1–84782–069–3

O1 170 192 9

Published by
F. A. Thorpe (Publishing)
Anstey, Leicestershire

Set by Words & Graphics Ltd.
Anstey, Leicestershire
Printed and bound in Great Britain by
T. J. International Ltd., Padstow, Cornwall

This book is printed on acid-free paper

Contents

Introduction

A schoolboy of fourteen at the turn of the twentieth and twenty-first centuries finds himself impelled to write stories about Sherlock Holmes, the Great Detective, more than a hundred years after Arthur Conan Doyle first brought him to life. And, if these four tales are not perfect in every detail — as one who has written the occasional Holmes pastiche myself, I know how extremely difficult it is to get everything right — they certainly achieve the first fundamental necessity.

They tell a story. You may raise an eyebrow from time to time at some chronological gaffe — train seats allocated in advance in a wholly twenty-first-century manner — but nevertheless you read on. You come to the point in the story *The Three-faced Villain* where Holmes asservates that the butler plays his Mistress's piano, and you have to rush on to discover how the great man can make such an outrageous assertion without having heard the least tinkle of melodious notes. Then just a few lines further on Edmund Hastie gives you the answer. The creasing of the upper part of the trouser leg from the piano stool.

I suppose, knowing the age of the author, one may be inclined to doubt the flawless logic here. But, pause, didn't Conan Doyle himself produce Holmesian logic every bit as open to cynical doubt? The dog in the night-time might very well have failed to bark simply because it had eaten a good dinner and was sleeping like a log. But Doyle slides you past any such doubts by the sheer rightness of the words. And, if his hundred-years-on young successor doesn't quite always do that, he generally comes close enough.

Take in *A Wilful Case* his phrase *it is the most venomous creature on earth*. There is the genuine sweeping claim that defies disbelief, as did Doyle's equally bland statement in *The Speckled Band* that the swamp adder is the deadliest snake in India. It ain't. It doesn't even exist. But as you read you believe in every inch of the peculiar yellow band with the brownish speckles eventually bound tightly round the head of the murderous Dr Grimesby Roylott. So, equally, do you give credit to Edmund Hastie's South American Poison Arrow Frog.

The book is, in short, a triumph. Not, alas, altogether for Edmund Hastie. How could a fourteen-year-old hope wholly to emulate one of the finest writers of his day? But the young author has done well enough: the stories are there, plenty of contemporaneous touches light up the pages and, above all, Sherlock Holmes is present in all his characteristic arrogance (if with a touch more bad-temper than I remember) and all his inevitability of success. No, the real triumph is that after so many years Doyle's Great Detective has succeeded in invading the mind of a twenty-first-century schoolboy so powerfully that these four stories have come to happy life.

H.R.F. Keating, May 2000

The Disappearing Prince

After a brief recollection of the multitude of cases I have chronicled, I find some which, at the time, appeared to be Holmes's greatest challenge yet and others which seemed to be profoundly simple. Every other case of daring and danger Holmes had previously undertaken was as nothing compared with the one I shall relate presently. It is the only case that Holmes (and myself) ever undertook where all our witnesses or informants entertained not the slightest hope of any success whatsoever. Speed, time and surprise were our most valuable allies in this case. Holmes's rapid deductions and his profound knowledge of such a vast array of unexpected material were equally vital to the eventual success of our mission.

If my memory serves me correctly, the events I am about to relate took place at the beginning of the year 1904. I was sipping rather cautiously at some piping hot punch which Holmes had kindly prepared for me. Christmas had only recently passed, so that the season of goodwill was a very pleasant memory, while winter weather always offered a perfect excuse to indulge my weakness for Holmes's special punch. I was inhaling its pungent aroma, when there was a short, sharp knock at the door and Mrs Hudson, Holmes's landlady, entered with a telegram for him. Once she had delivered it, she left the room. Holmes quickly opened it, read it through to himself, then catching my eye, addressed me.

'This telegram, Watson, is from a very old friend of mine, whom I have unfortunately seldom had time to meet in the last decade or so, though His Majesty's postal service has kept us in touch as on this occasion. I have known him since we were at school together. He is now the Professor of Classics at one of the two most illustrious and ancient seats of learning in this sceptred isle of ours. He is also the Warden of King Athelstan's College there.

'He informs me, and this is in the strictest confidence, Watson, that the Crown Prince of Japan has disappeared from his college rooms. According to my friend, who can be relied upon, there was no sign whatsoever of any struggle, yet he has nameless fears on this young man's behalf and wishes me to find him as quickly as possible.'

'Whatever was the Crown Prince of Japan doing at one of our most eminent institutions of learning?' I enquired.

'Watson, you amaze me. You are obviously tired. Or, perhaps, my special punch has addled your brain. It is not to be doubted that the young man was imbibing the advanced scientific knowledge that we in the West have to offer. Japan is determined to avoid being colonized and so must modernize. It appears that the Crown Prince was at King Athelstan's College as an under-graduate student of the physical sciences,' explained Holmes, rather aghast that I should be so ignorant of such a seemingly obvious fact. 'Come, Watson, let us hurry. I have an intuition that time is definitely not on our side in this case,' he added.

I threw a few personal possessions into a bag. Within a few minutes Holmes and myself were fully kitted out for our excursion to a city a few counties north of London. I took the precaution of finishing my glass of punch, albeit hurriedly, before we departed.

'We look more like Arctic explorers, rather than travellers heading a few miles northward,' chuckled Holmes. Then picking up on the subject of the Arctic, 'Well, Captain Scott, what is it like to travel a few miles north of civilization?' he asked with a roguish twinkle in his eye.

'Painful,' I answered, with a woeful shake of my head.

We left Baker Street chuckling quietly to ourselves, and after a brisk journey in a cab we arrived at one of London's many rail terminuses. We boarded the train on platform 4, which Holmes assured me was the one we required. We were soon speeding away from London. A few picturesque English counties later, we arrived at our destination. Upon alighting on the station platform, a slightly built gentleman, wearing a greatcoat that indicated the fashion of a bygone era, hurried up to Holmes.

'Horace!' exclaimed Holmes, shaking his hand warmly. Clapping his hand on my shoulder, he added, 'This is my friend and companion, Dr Watson, who can be trusted with any secret you care to name. You may speak freely in his presence for he is the soul of discretion.'

We left the station where a horse-drawn carriage was waiting to take us to the college.

Once we were in Professor Horace Small's study, he explained that it was imperative that the police should not be alerted.

'That is the reason I have called you in, Holmes. The involvement of the police will alert the gentlemen of the press and create such a scandal that no foreign dignitaries will ever again trust their offspring to the educational care of King Athelstan's. This institution's reputation will be damaged beyond repair. In any case, the disappearance may well have an innocent explanation, which I fervently hope, and if that turns out to be the case, there is even less reason to alarm the police.'

'Can you tell us something about this young prince? Is he a thoughtless gadabout?'

'Certainly not!' Professor Small replied. 'The young prince is a dutiful, diligent student. His tutors think most highly of him. He appears not to give in to any of the temptations that young men removed from parental authority can sometimes find hard to resist. He is here in the West to learn all that we have to teach about science. Previously, he had never left the college grounds for more than a few hours without informing someone in authority of his destination and possible time of return.'

Holmes nodded assent, then asked, 'Horace, my dear fellow, would it be possible for us to see the room the Crown Prince lives in?'

'Certainly,' answered Professor Small.

He took us across the quadrangle to a small entrance immediately opposite the windows of his own accommodation. We ascended a staircase, at the top of which we turned and proceeded down a corridor. Eventually Professor Small stopped, fished a key from his pocket and unlocked the door.

'Why do you lock the door?' I enquired.

'In case some friend of his comes along, goes in and realizes that he is not there. I would have some explaining to do then.'

Once we were within the room, he re-locked the door from the inside. It was basically a study with a bed in one corner. Behind every other door along the same corridor would be found similar accommodation. Though he was the Crown Prince and would one day be the Emperor of Japan, his father had insisted that he should be treated like every other student at the college.

The fireplace was out of proportion with the rest of the room, for it was so very large. On the mantelpiece stood some small trophies. There was a deep, red leather armchair at the side of it. The hearth had not yet been cleaned and was

11

full of the charred remains of a recent fire. A large mahogany desk and swivel chair were positioned by the window, so that when the occupant was working at the desk and glanced up, his gaze would be soothed by the broad expanse of the university gardens with their classical landscaping and mature trees. The top of the desk was tidy, with a polished brass inkstand and two pens resting in its tray. Adjacent to it was a silver box. There was a finished essay, ready to be handed in, on one side of the desk and on the other side was ample fresh stationery arranged in an orderly pile. Beside the desk was a cane waste-paper basket containing a few discarded pieces of paper.

Stretching along the whole length of one wall was a handsome bookcase, containing many volumes bound in leather. A rather faded, but capacious, carpet covered most of the wooden floorboards. The bed had not been slept in and looked rather simple for the son and heir of the Japanese Emperor.

Holmes did not pay much attention to the bed, apart from noting the fact that it had not been slept in. Stooping over the hearth, he was far more preoccupied with the grate. He strode over to the desk, opened the silver box and briefly raised it to within several inches of his nose. Then he returned to the hearth where he used his penknife to pick up a flake or two of the ash that had fallen there.

'Aha!' he exclaimed, holding before us the ashy remains of what he declared had been the fag-end of a cigarette that had been dropped into the hearth. He sniffed the ash, then carefully examined it.

'This is the remains of a cigarette of a very particular and distinctive kind, thrown away not by the Crown Prince, but by a visitor. It is Russian,' he declared holding the ash up to the light. 'I am familiar with twenty-four different varieties of tobacco leaf. This particular cigarette was grown on the shores of the Caspian Sea some two or three years heretofore. I would venture to say it was rolled in Minsk. It is a most suspicious find, seeing that the Crown Prince does not smoke Russian cigarettes,' he declared emphatically.

'How have you deduced that?' Professor Small and I asked at the same time.

'The silver cigarette box on the desk contains the finest Virginia cigarettes, which presumably are the ones the Crown Prince prefers for himself. I conclude, therefore, that this Russian cigarette must have been smoked by a visitor to his room.'

Turning to Professor Small, he enquired, 'All visitors have to sign the visitors' book, I suppose?' which his friend confirmed was so. 'I wish to see it,' Holmes stated.

Professor Small departed to find the visitors' book kept at the porter's lodge. In the meantime, Holmes suddenly dropped on one knee on the carpet and scraped up a few pieces of dried soil, which he put in an envelope he took from his pocket.

'This will prove useful,' he declared.

'Have you reached any conclusions which might explain the Crown Prince's disappearance?' I enquired.

'Yes, Watson, I have. The Crown Prince was abducted.'

'Abducted!' I exclaimed in absolute horror.

'Or kidnapped.'

'Kidnapped!' I echoed in disbelief.

'My dear Watson, could you possibly make your exclamations a little less audible to people at the end of the corridor? I have no wish for Professor Small to hear, for he would be most distressed. And possibly in his distress blurt out this whole disagreeable business to an unsuspecting comforter. So, Watson, for the first and last time, contain yourself,' commanded Holmes.

A few minutes later Professor Small returned with a list of the names and addresses of the visitors the Crown Prince had received during the week before his strange disappearance.

Holmes scanned the list. His eyes stopped on one of the names. He grabbed his friend by the arm and asked him, 'Have you ever met this man, Horace?'

'Yes, I have the honour to be acquainted with him, for he is a most pleasant and polite young gentleman. He was at Harrow with the Crown Prince and they are the best of friends. I can remember very little about him except that he had a slight foreign accent.'

'I expected he would have,' replied Holmes with a smile. 'With a surname like Czapiezci, he is hardly likely to be English, is he? Did you see him leave the Crown Prince's rooms yesterday?'

'I didn't and none of my colleagues did either. I visited the Crown Prince's room an hour later and found his room empty. I sent you a telegram instantly.'

Holmes frowned, folded up the piece of paper with the list on it and thrust it into his jacket pocket. Then as if something had just struck him, he strode over to the wardrobe and flung the double doors wide open.

'Aha! His rowing gloves aren't here.'

'What have rowing gloves to do with the case?' I asked, baffled.

'Watson, my dear fellow, observation is of the essence in detection. Just look at the trophies and medals on the mantelpiece. They were all awarded to him for rowing.'

Holmes closed the wardrobe doors,

then sat down heavily in the chair by the desk. He snatched up the waste-paper basket and rummaged inside it. He removed a small scrunched-up ball of paper, opened it out, read it and put it into his pocket.

Leaping up, he said, 'Come, Watson, follow me. Horace, lock the room up again.'

Holmes strode quickly from the room into the corridor. As I followed his brisk walk out of the university building, I marvelled at how he never paused to wait for me and to ponder if he was heading towards the correct way out of the labyrinth. Eventually we emerged into the sunlight. Holmes handed me the paper which had been screwed up and thrown into the waste-paper basket and bade me read it. I opened it out and read the message written on it in pencil. It read as follows: 'Meet me with 249 at half past three tomorrow afternoon. Yours, A.B.'

I wondered who this A.B. could be, but now I did not wonder why we were going to the boathouse. Holmes took the paper back.

'It is a great pity that the note has no date. We would be able to link the Crown Prince's disappearance with its arrival far more easily. This note could have arrived a fortnight ago or a week before his disappearance. If it did so, its worth is considerably reduced, probably useless. However, we must investigate.'

We arrived at the boathouse and were greeted by the boatkeeper, who, judging from his accent, was a Norfolk man.

'I wish to make some inquiries,' stated Holmes. 'If you assist us, you shall be rewarded. If you choose not to, you will not be financially assisted in any way whatsoever. Is that clear?'

The boatkeeper nodded assent.

'If students at the college row here, are they given their own boats for the duration of their time at this university?'

'Yes, sir, if they join the rowing club, they are.'

'Has the Crown Prince joined and been allotted a boat?' Holmes continued.

'He has indeed, sir. It is number 249, at least I think it is. Wait here, sir, while I go and check.'

He disappeared inside the boathouse. 'It *is* 249, sir,' he declared from inside a few moments later. Then we heard a steady tapping of footsteps fade away, then presently return again. The boatkeeper emerged from the long shed. 'I'm sorry, sir, but the Crown Prince's boat isn't there.'

'Thank you for your information. You have been most helpful. Now my colleague and I wish to take a turn on the river. I trust you will oblige?' asked Holmes, holding out a shilling. 'We will take boat number 248.'

'Certainly, sir,' the boatkeeper answered, touching the rim of his cap respectfully. We followed him into the boathouse and were escorted to the mooring farthest away from the entrance. As we clambered aboard the boat I observed that the decking of the landing stage had the number 248 painted on it, but there was no boat tied up where the number 249 was painted.

As our boat was being cast off, the boatkeeper enquired, 'Are you gentlemen at university here?'

'Yes, indirectly so,' answered Holmes,

an answer which seemed to reassure the boatkeeper and he saluted us cheerily as we moved away from the mooring.

I had taken the tiller and Holmes the oars. Once we had cleared some way from the boathouse, Holmes gently sculled. 'Don't you think this is bliss, Watson,' Holmes enquired, 'with the gentle melodious sound of the water lapping against the bow of the boat?'

'Absolutely, Holmes,' I uttered.

'Presently, however, Watson, I am going to splash a bit to prevent any passerby from overhearing our conversation.'

A few hundred yards or so later, Holmes began to splash his oars into the water fiercely, making the water foam around us.

'There are so many intricate strands in this case, Watson, I fear it may be near impossible to string them all together. In short, I feel that this case has grown cold.'

'I am less inclined to think so, Holmes,' I argued.

'Really!' exclaimed Holmes. 'Do you have to reject every statement I make?' shaking his head in displeasure. 'Let me state the facts and series of events to you, then you may make a balanced suggestion towards the future possibilities of this case. Firstly, Watson, the Crown Prince of Japan, one of our allies and trading partners, has disappeared. There was no sign whatsoever of a struggle. All his visitors were fellow students, even that friend with the mysterious name, who, I suspect, is not Russian. Czapiezci is a Slavic name, but I am inclined to think it is Polish. As you are no doubt aware, the Poles are under the Russian yoke, so will therefore not give them the slightest assistance. In fact, the Poles will be more likely to hinder the Russians rather than help them. Therefore, Watson, I do not feel justified in suspecting him. My suspicions have shifted.'

'In the direction of A.B.?' I enquired.

'Precisely, Watson. The initials on the telegram.'

Holmes then rowed back to the boathouse where he gave the delighted boatkeeper half a sovereign. We made our way back to the university to make further inquiries. Upon arriving back in

Professor Small's rooms Holmes asked about the initials A.B.

'On the list that you gave me of the Crown Prince's recent visitors there are two names with the initials A.B. — Alfred Billington and Archie Blair. What can you tell me about these two students, Horace?'

'Alfred Billington has been in hospital since last week with a broken leg. Lord Archibald Blair is a much respected undergraduate at St Perpetua's College and his father was recently raised to the peerage. That is all I know. But the Master of his college would know more.'

'Let us go, then,' Holmes urged.

Since this college was a short walk from King Athelstan's college, it was not long before we were sitting in the Master's rooms. Professor Small informed him of the reason for the presence of the great detective, his old friend Sherlock Holmes, and swore him to complete secrecy. Holmes began.

'Sir Bertrand, I would be grateful if you could answer some questions I am going to put to you. What do you know about

Lord Archibald Blair other than his academic achievements?'

'He is new money. His Scottish father made his fortune importing furs from Russia. In fact, his ships dominated the Baltic run from Dundee to Russia for many years, I do believe.'

'There! Holmes, that is surely explanation enough to justify the presence of Russian tobacco in the room,' Horace Small commented. 'As a man of wealth and Russian trading contacts, Lord Blair would come by such goods easily.'

'But doesn't that mean that the trail has gone cold, Holmes?' I enquired.

'Quite the contrary!' snapped Holmes. 'The Russian connection only confirms my suspicions. Sir Bertrand, do you have any inkling of this young man's political leanings? If he has taken sides with the Russian Bear in its present tussle with the Japanese, that would not bode well for the Crown Prince.'

'That is a very interesting question and your suspicions are correct. Whatever the Russians do, he sides with them. Only the other day, he was overheard in the junior common room condemning the Japanese actions against Russia in the Far East.'

Sir Bertrand then began to ask some questions of his own. 'Do you think that a ransom will be demanded for the Crown Prince's safe return?'

'As Lord Archibald has no need of money, I am forced to conclude that this escapade is conducted out of misguided political idealism. Taking sides is never a wise course. As here, it may mean the betrayal of a friend. If he is working for the Russians then Japanese withdrawal from Russian territory may be the price of the Crown Prince's release. As time is not on our side, we must now make our way to the library, to check tide maps and coastal charts.'

'East Anglia has rather a long coast-line,' Sir Bertrand reminded us as we made our way to the door.

Upon reaching the university buildings we proceeded immediately to the library. Holmes headed for the map section and began examining a map of the surrounding counties.

Looking up at me as I stood beside

him, he said, 'We rowed upstream on the river Cam. Its banks showed no signs of any presence of people, nor any recent evidence of boats. In short, there were no footprints nor signs of any boats being tied up or pulled ashore. This means that the Crown Prince rowed downstream to meet Lord Archibald Blair. If the Crown Prince's boat is to be found, it will be discovered downstream, not upstream. The Cam is a tributary of the larger confluence, the Ouse, that leads to the quiet, old fishing port of King's Lynn, the perfect place from which to 'export' a young man without attracting attention.

'The Russians will have taken the Crown Prince from King's Lynn into the Wash where, no doubt, a Russian fishing vessel will be waiting for their arrival. The Crown Prince will then be taken to Russia, where he will be used as a bargaining counter to force the Japanese to leave Manchuria, which they invaded earlier this year. The Japanese have achieved a series of stunning victories against the Russians. That is the reason why his disappearance has taken place. It is a well contrived plan. If we fail in our duty to recover him, there will be a series of repercussions which will not be forgotten for generations to come,' stated Holmes. 'If we are to rescue the Crown Prince, Watson, we must not stay here. We must search farther afield.'

'But where?' I enquired.

'To King's Lynn, of course,' answered Holmes.

We left the university for the railway station. Holmes purchased two first-class tickets and we were soon rattling away to King's Lynn. A few shady, sceptred shires later, we arrived at the resort of King's Lynn. From the station we took a cab to the harbour. When our cab had departed, Holmes and I looked out to sea, while he explained why we were there.

'Whilst you were idly wandering amongst the multitude of mellowed volumes in the university library, I was memorizing the tides in the Wash. The next high tide is in ten minutes.'

We waited patiently for that moment to arrive while Holmes kept looking down at his watch. When the time was up, he snapped his pocket watch shut and then scanned the horizon.

'Look! Look! Watson!' he exclaimed. 'A Russian fishing vessel! It is pleasing to know that they are on time. I absolutely detest criminals who are late! Now that we have ascertained that the Crown Prince will be removed from this country tonight, let us act swiftly to prevent that happening. We can do nothing here, so let us head for the most northern point of the harbour and lie in wait there where we shall be able to see all the boats going in and out of it.'

We made our way there and from our vantage point we had a clear view over most of the harbour. Dusk fell and the Russian fishing vessel, whose arrival we had been expecting for some time, finally hove towards the shore. It pulled up close to the side of the harbour we were hiding on. Directly opposite us three men were hurrying along the quayside carrying a long, heavy sack. They clambered into a small rowing boat and rowed away from the quayside towards the Russian ketch.

Holmes burst out of our place of concealment, took his revolver from his pocket and fired once. This shot hit the man with the oars in the shoulder. Another man took his place at the oars. Holmes took careful aim, then fired again. This time the man rowing was wounded in the hand.

'I see no good reason to kill them for we need survivors for evidence,' remarked Holmes. The injury to the man's hand was obviously causing him some distress. He was unable to row properly with one hand and the boat was going round and round in circles. The remaining man in the boat snatched the oars and began rowing furiously towards the Russian ketch.

'Stop!' bellowed Holmes. 'If you value your lives, row over to us now! Move!'

They obeyed. When their boat came up to the quayside, Holmes boarded her and grabbed the mass of sacking. I covered Holmes with his revolver while he slit the sacking open with his penknife, taking care not to hurt the person inside. Presently all the sacking had been removed and apart from looking pale and a little flustered, the Crown Prince appeared quite well.

Very soon after this, drawn by the noise of Holmes's two revolver shots, two policemen came running along the quay.

'Evenin', gentlemen. What's going on here?' said the older of the two constables.

'You will arrest those three men in the boat,' ordered Holmes in a convincing tone of authority. 'Then alert the coastguards to board that Russian vessel, arrest every single crew member and intern the boat.'

'Just a moment, sir. Just who do you think you are?' demanded the constable who had first spoken to them.

'Who do *I* think I am?' enquired Holmes. 'Who do *you* think I am?'

The policeman moved closer to Holmes and looked at him searchingly. 'Oh, I beg your pardon, Mr Holmes. I didn't recognize you in this light.'

'Very well. Carry out my instructions to the letter and I shall mention you favourably to Scotland Yard.'

The Crown Prince was a little unsteady on his legs at first but we managed to walk along the quay till we hailed a cab. We were driven to the station where we were just in time to catch a train to the university town. A cab took us from the station to King Athelstan's College. We escorted the Crown Prince to Professor Small's study where he was delighted to see all three of us. He arranged a supper for the Crown Prince and after he had eaten ordered him to go to his room and lock himself inside; an order he was only too pleased to obey.

Having seen the Crown Prince safely to his room, Holmes stated his wish to visit Lord Archibald Blair. After signing the visitors' book, we were directed to his rooms. Holmes paused outside the door and examined the boots left there for cleaning. The soles were caked with mud. Holmes smiled. After his examination, he rapped on the door and waited for a response, tapping his foot on the floor. Eventually an answer came. The door was opened and Holmes and I swept in.

'Judas!' exclaimed Holmes the moment

I had closed the door behind us.

'Kindly explain the reason for this unseemly intrusion, sir!' bellowed Lord Archibald Blair.

'This intrusion, young man,' said Holmes, 'is to inform you that I have found you out!'

Lord Blair stared at him, then turned to me. 'Are you perhaps his keeper, sir?' he asked me. 'For the fellow is clearly in no state to be allowed out alone!'

It was Holmes's turn to stare. 'My name is Sherlock Holmes,' he said, 'and it would be better for you to answer my questions. Do you deny being implicated in the abduction of the Crown Prince of Japan?'

'Of course I deny it!' said Lord Blair, adding to me, 'I was right first time about this chap!'

'But you cannot deny being in the Crown Prince's rooms yesterday,' said Holmes. 'The earth I found on his carpet is the terracotta quite characteristic of St Perpetua's and nowhere else in the university. That, taken with your distinctive Russian cigarettes, places you in the Prince's rooms.'

Lord Blair shrugged. 'I do not deny it for a moment. But what of it?'

'Why were you there?' asked Holmes.

'The Prince invited me there for a drink and a talk. We did not see eye to eye on political matters — '

'Ahah! So you do not deny that?' asked Holmes.

'Again, there is no reason why I should do so,' pointed out Lord Blair. 'But it is no crime to hold opinions contrary to those of another man.'

'And so you accompanied the Prince to his rooms, where you talked? And nothing more?'

'We talked for a short time, then the Prince said that I must excuse him, as he had a prior engagement.'

'What time was that?'

'Oh — three o'clock? About then.'

'And you then left the Prince?'

'I did,' said Blair.

'Where did you go?'

Blair gave a shamefaced grin. 'I worked, hard though that may be to believe of an undergraduate at St Perpetua's! As a matter of fact, I had a

Classics tutorial with Professor Small. We got talking and it lasted until almost time for supper.'

'Professor Small failed to mention that fact!' said Holmes, nettled.

Blair shrugged his shoulders.

I answered for him. 'Why should he?' I asked Holmes. 'You did not ask Professor Small his whereabouts on the day in question, after all!'

Holmes smiled. 'You are right, Watson.' Yet he looked baffled by all this. To Blair, he said, 'But you were by the river recently. That much is apparent from my study of your boots.'

Blair nodded. 'I row, like many of the men here. What of that?'

Holmes sank back in his chair. 'Can it be that I have missed something?' he mused, half to himself. 'There were but two visitors with the initials 'A.B.', and the other, Billington, is in hospital with a broken leg.'

'What, Freddie Billington of King Athelstan's?' asked Blair. 'He isn't, you know. That is, he has a broken leg all right, or at any rate he sports a massive plaster cast, but he isn't in hospital. He's back in his rooms, for I spotted him there just this morning, and he told me he'd been released, or whatever you call it, a couple of days ago. Oh — ' he added, for Holmes was on his feet and out of the door almost before Lord Blair had finished.

I made some hasty mumbled apology, and followed Holmes, who led me to King Athelstan's, where he enquired of the porter the whereabouts of Alfred Billington's rooms.

Holmes raced up the narrow stairs, along a corridor, and tapped on the door of the rooms the porter had indicated. Without waiting for any invitation, he threw the door open almost as he tapped upon it.

I had a sort of vague impression of a sudden flurry of movement within the room, but when I followed Holmes inside, the sole occupant proved to be a handsome though rather sulky young man, who sat in a chair. One leg was stuck out before him, a great plaster cast on it. Were it not rankly impossible, I should have said that the young man had thrown himself hastily into the chair as Holmes burst into the room!

However, he greeted us civilly enough. 'Gentlemen, to what do I owe this delightful visit?'

'Mr Alfred Billington, I believe? My name is Sherlock Holmes, and you may find that the visit is not quite as delightful as you would wish!'

Mr Billington frowned. 'I hardly follow you, Mr Holmes. I have heard of your exploits, of course. Who has not? But I fear — '

Holmes silenced him with a hand held up. 'Your leg does not trouble you too much, I fancy?'

'Not too much. It makes it impossible to move around as I would like, of course.'

'Indeed,' said Holmes. 'Such a monstrous cast would slow down an elephant! What say you, Watson?'

'It has certainly been very clumsily done,' I said. 'Had one of my old dressers made so heavy-handed a job of it, I should have had something to say!'

'Perhaps my colleague here might examine your cast?' said Holmes.

'No, no! That is, there is no need, I assure you. Perfectly fine, perfectly comfortable — '

'Indeed? My own expertise lies in a different direction,' said Holmes, 'so with your permission I shall merely examine the boots which I see in the corner there.'

As Billington and I watched in astonishment, Holmes strolled over and picked up the boots he had indicated.

'You say you have not been able to get about with the cast on your leg?'

'That is correct. Out of action this past week.'

'Indeed?' said Holmes again. 'Then how is it that there is perfectly fresh mud, deposited no earlier than two days ago, as I judge — and I am something of an expert — upon not just one, but on both, of these boots?'

Billington shrugged his shoulders, and leaned forward. I assumed his leg was tickling, and he was trying to scratch under the plaster, something I have often witnessed in such cases. But to my considerable astonishment he removed the entire cast, which I now saw was a fake, a theatrical 'prop'! Before either of us had properly realized what was happening, Billington had thrown the cast at Holmes, who was obliged to duck out of the way, losing his footing as he did so. Meantime, Billington himself leaped to his feet and made for the door.

I was never much of an oarsman myself in my time at university, but I was a pretty useful rugby forward. I dived for Billington's legs, and brought him down in one of the finest tackles of my career.

'Well done, Watson!' said Holmes with approval, slipping his handcuffs on to Billington's wrists. 'If you would further oblige me by ringing for the porter, and ask him to call a policeman?'

'But why did you do it?' I asked Billington. 'Lord Blair I could understand, his political antipathy to the Prince, and so on, but what was your motive?'

He did not reply, but merely sat in sullen silence. It was Holmes who answered me. 'I fancy, Watson, that it was one of the oldest reasons of all — money. There are many temptations, expensive temptations, for a young man at college. Cards, slow horses, fast women.'

'Too true!' I said, with a reminiscent sigh.

Holmes frowned.

'Sorry, Holmes. But which is it?'

'Perhaps Mr Billington would enliven the journey to the cells, which would otherwise be somewhat tedious and menacing for him, by recounting the precise details to us? No? No matter. It will all come out at the trial! Watson, the porter, if you would?'

A Wilful Case

It was a dank and dismal evening. The rain lashed incessantly at the window panes. Sherlock Holmes gazed solemnly out of the window with an expression of extreme perplexity and boredom. I was on the point of asking if I should leave when he suddenly murmured, 'Don't you think, my dear Watson, that life is so infinitely boring when there isn't a case to solve?'

'Well, at least someone isn't being murdered, robbed, swindled or cheated out of anything,' I replied.

Holmes gave a deep sigh, rolled his eyes twice, gritted his teeth and replied quite slowly, 'My dear Watson, if you think that because there is a slight lull in the number of clients I am receiving at the moment, you are very much mistaken indeed.'

His tone, though sharp, was not unkind. In spite of his somewhat abrupt response, I continued to press my case.

'But surely, if there was a problem, the victim, or widow or widower, would come to you for advice, wouldn't they?'

'Not necessarily. Out of all the wrongs that people have done to them precious few will regard them as bad enough to inform me of them. And besides, not everyone who has been wronged knows of my existence, so therefore will be unable to come to me.'

I had to agree that there was something in what he was saying, but I had no intention of backing down. Before I could even reply to his rebuttal, he said quite solemnly, 'Watson, there are points on both our sides and I feel that should we continue to disagree on this topic, it will merely undermine our friendship, something that I have no wish to do.'

'And I have no wish to undermine our friendship either,' I replied, somewhat less solemnly than he had made his little speech.

Sherlock Holmes glanced up at the gilded clock on the mantelpiece and yawned. This was followed by a sharp knock at the door. He looked somewhat startled that he might have a client outside. He strolled over to the door, as casually as ever, and opened it with the gentlemanly ease that I had always known him to exhibit during the lengthy period that we had been friends.

Into the room stepped a tall, fair and somewhat shy young lady. Holmes motioned her to be seated in one of his armchairs. She seated herself without the least hesitation, while Holmes stood with his back to the fire. The lady fumbled in her handbag for a moment and then drew out a handkerchief with which she dabbed her eyes a few times. As a doctor I could not help noticing how very red and inflamed her eyes were. It was obvious that she had been crying in abundance lately.

Holmes took a deep breath and then began to address the lady in a most familiar tone.

'My dear Mrs Jane Wiggold, was it not a rather long and tiresome journey, all the way from Nightingale Lane?'

'Yes, it was rather,' she replied, then straightening up with a start, gulped, blinked a few times, then looked up at Holmes and whispered in a shaky voice, 'How did you know that?'

Holmes chuckled to himself then explained, 'While you were searching for your handkerchief, I took the liberty of peering into your bag. Your address was embroidered most clearly, if I may say so, onto the inside of your bag, so when you opened it, I could read it perfectly. As to your name, it is embroidered in blue upon your handkerchief.'

'Well, well,' uttered Mrs Wiggold. 'It's so very simple once you explain it to me.'

'It is mere observation,' replied Holmes. 'I trust that you have come here to ask advice, not merely to marvel at my powers of observation!'

'Well, Mr Holmes, I trust that you will not think it silly or improper that I should call on you in this way. I hope and believe that you will not find my story too complex or unbelievable that you will not tackle it.'

'I cannot decide if I shall tackle your case if I haven't heard it,' replied Holmes. 'Tell me the facts in the exact order that they occurred. Feel free to include any little facts, even if you may think them trivial and of no real importance. They may be the vital clues that I must search for. Pause only to take breath, nothing more. Now, please, disclose your story to me.'

Mrs Wiggold wrung her hands together for a moment, then began her narrative.

'You see, Mr Holmes, my father married for money and solely for money. My mother was completely unaware of this when she married him. She was an heiress to a vast fortune of which I know not what the original sum was. When her father died, the couple were married six months later, after my mother had ceased to mourn her beloved father. My grandfather had only one child, who was my mother, so the entire fortune passed to her. My father was not included in Grandfather's will, so naturally received nothing. He was, fortunately enough he thought, married to the sole receiver of my grandfather's wealth. He began to beg my mother for some of the money she had inherited. Naturally she gave him some, but he still wanted more. My mother began to dislike him but naturally enough didn't show it in case that would hurt his feelings. It was about this time that my mother realized that her husband had married her not for love but for her money. She was quite sickened by this realization. The next day she went to her lawyers and made a will where the entire fortune would be left to my older brother with smaller sums to be left to my other older brother and to myself. Nothing was to be left for my father.'

'Nothing for your father?' asked Holmes.

'Nothing at all,' replied Mrs Wiggold.

'Why nothing at all?' enquired Holmes.

'My mother said that because he had done nothing for her and she had given so much money to him already, she didn't see why she should give him anything else.'

'I understand,' muttered Holmes. 'Pray continue with your story.'

Mrs Wiggold coughed once, then went on.

'A week after Mother made out her will, she died at work. Our doctor explained to me that she might have been poisoned. On hearing this, I was naturally thrown into a state of extreme distress, worry and suspicion. I say suspicion but I had no idea who could have killed her.'

'Quite so,' remarked Holmes. 'Pray continue.'

'My eldest brother made out his will, in case anything happened to him. The family fortune was to be divided between my other brother and myself with nothing, you understand, to be left to my father.'

'I understand perfectly,' stated Holmes.

'A week later my eldest brother was fished out of the Thames.' At this point Mrs Wiggold sobbed and blew her nose a few times into her handkerchief. I could see how most exasperating Holmes found all this. He rolled his eyes towards the ceiling, gritted his teeth and began quietly to huff and puff.

Eventually Mrs Wiggold's sobbing ceased and Holmes addressed her.

'Mrs Wiggold, I trust that you and your brother have both made wills stating to whom the rest of the fortune should be given in the event of your deaths.'

'Oh, yes,' Mrs Wiggold assured him. 'My brother and I made out our wills yesterday. We both agreed that we should leave the fortune to a person that my father did not know existed, namely, my husband. We knew for a fact that my father had not the least knowledge of my husband's existence and therefore — '

'How did you know your father had no knowledge of your husband's existence?' Holmes interrupted.

'He keeps on imploring me to get married. The last time he did so was yesterday, so he cannot possibly suspect that I am married already. Only my mother, my late brother and his younger brother knew. We were married in secret, you see, so that my father wouldn't have any knowledge of it.'

'My, my, what a very strange and secretive family you all are. On hearing your narrative I feel sure that you believe your father to be the sole culprit. You wish me to discover who murdered your mother and your eldest brother. Is that correct?'

'Quite so. And now, Mr Holmes,' she uttered, 'I must go. Father will suspect something if I stay any longer. There is a spare key under the doormat, Mr Holmes, should you require to search my father's room for any evidence you may think relevant. Father goes to his club most afternoons, so you can slip into the house when he is out. I am at work most of the day but I am always back in the evenings.'

'Do you enjoy playing the piano?' asked Holmes.

Mrs Wiggold gave a start, then glared at Holmes.

'All right, Mr Holmes, how do you know that I'm a pianist?' she demanded.

'Really,' grumbled Holmes, 'I never cease to marvel at the complete ignorance of some of my clients. To answer your question, Mrs Wiggold, the bridge of your nose shows very clearly the marks left by your spectacles, so you obviously do close work. Secondly, when you were fumbling in your handbag I noticed how very agile your fingers were. Your fingers pushed the unwanted articles to either side of the bag, then you took out your handkerchief. Agile fingers means two things. You are either a pianist or a dressmaker. If you were a pianist, your fingers would have flat tips which they quite noticably do, so you are a pianist.'

'Oh yes, I see now,' replied a rather bewildered Mrs Wiggold.

'If you call again in two or three days, I may have some information for you.'

'Thank you, Mr Holmes. I hope and believe that you will bring the murderer to justice. Goodbye, Mr Holmes,' whispered Mrs Wiggold.

'I hope so, too,' retorted Holmes. He opened the door and she glided out as though she were on skates. He closed the door in his usual crisp way, then crossed the room and turned down the lamp. Having done so, he stepped quickly to the window.

'Aha, a brougham! Well, well,' remarked Holmes to me. 'Is it hers though? Aha, it is! Well, well, I wonder how a pianist could possibly afford any carriage, let alone a brougham. There is something most suspicious about her as well as about this case.'

'Holmes, it is late,' I stated. 'I think I had better leave now. My wife will be worried if I stay away much longer.'

'Quite so,' replied Holmes. 'I understand perfectly. By the way, Watson, I hope that you will be able to come back here tomorrow. Shall we say six in the evening?'

I nodded assent, wished him goodnight and left his apartment. As I trundled home in a hansom cab, I could not help marvelling at the complexity of the case. I felt confident that Holmes would be able to unravel the mysteries surrounding this case with ease.

My day dragged slowly by, but eventually my patients had all been attended to and I was able to make my way to Baker Street. I arrived a few minutes early and hurried to Holmes's apartment. I found him smoking his old pipe.

'Ah, Watson,' he exclaimed as I closed the door. 'I think that this case will take me quite some time to fathom.'

'But you have your suspicions already?' I enquired.

'Oh, I always have my suspicions. It's my job. I wouldn't be a detective if I didn't have my suspicions.'

At this point, Holmes took a gulp of something that looked like water. Judging by his reaction on swallowing the first gulp, I realized that it was evidently something far stronger than mere water.

'This particular case has no end of possibilities as to who the culprit might be. When the mother died, the eldest son would benefit; when the eldest son died, the younger son would benefit; if the younger son dies, the daughter and her husband will benefit; if the daughter dies, then the husband will benefit again. In none of these instances does the father benefit. That does not, however, guarantee his innocence. I do find it somewhat hard to believe that any father could possibly kill his wife, then his eldest son. I assume it will be someone who is acquainted distantly with the family or perhaps an old enemy. As I said before I have no real evidence to go on, so I shall cease to make assumptions before I have any solid evidence.

'The eldest brother was murdered exactly a week after his mother. If the murderer is going to kill the remaining brother, then he will strike tomorrow. I am completely in the dark as to the method he will use. Also I am unaware of when he will strike.'

Sherlock Holmes then leapt out of his chair.

'Come on, Watson, we must hurry to Nightingale Lane as quickly as possible. I wish to do some ferreting around in Mrs Wiggold's house. There may be some clues there which will enable me to save her brother's life tomorrow.'

'What about her father? Surely he'll object to you rummaging about his house?'

'If he's a good father and he's innocent, he won't object in the least.'

That satisfied my curiosity, so I raced downstairs after Holmes. When I arrived in the street, I found him glancing up and down the street, searching for a cab. We both hurried to the end of Baker Street in the hope of finding a cab. Eventually out of the mist came a solitary hansom, its horse plodding along at the slowest possible speed.

'Cab!' bellowed Holmes at the top of his voice. 'Nightingale Lane. If you don't arrive there within the next twenty minutes, I shan't pay you!'

Eventually we arrived. I have never been so shaken before in my life. The cab rattled and shook so much that I would not have been in the least surprised if a few of my limbs had just separated themselves from my body. All my joints felt like those of a cripple. It was an unbelievable pleasure and joy to have solid ground beneath my feet again.

Holmes grabbed my arm and dragged me to the door of Mrs Wiggold's house. Finding the key under the doormat, we both slipped inside. We were standing in a large and airy entrance hall. There were several mahogany doors that lined the hall. Holmes opened the first door on the left and went in as noiselessly as he had come in through the front door. I followed him in. When we were both inside, he locked the door, crossed to the other side of the room and began to examine the papers on the desk. Meanwhile, I was sifting through the papers in the bureau which was to the left of the desk. After a minute or two had elapsed, Holmes whispered to me, 'It appears that Mrs Wiggold is biased against her father.'

'Quite so,' I whispered in reply.

'Did you notice, Watson, that during her account of the two deaths, she dropped hints that her father was guilty and even stated that she suspected his guilt, which makes me assume that she wants him to be convicted, even if he is innocent. I think that is why she told us the whereabouts of the house key in the hope that we might find some evidence that would convict him.'

I continued to search through the many papers inside the bureau. After I had read through all of them and found no information which was relevant to the case we were trying to solve, I decided that I should search the drawers of the bureau as well, in case they held any relevant information. The first drawer I opened contained only a large, red-covered book with the word 'Diary' printed in gold lettering on the front cover. It was the father's and this year's diary as well. I looked up the date when the mother had died. His account of what happened read as follows: 'Stayed inside all day. Wife tragically died at work. Jane told me of Mother's death at seven, when she came in from work. I was in deep shock and cried for hours. A great loss.'

Holmes crossed over to the bureau at this point.

'I have found absolutely nothing, Watson,' he grumbled in his usual dry manner. 'What's this, Watson?' he enquired. 'The father's diary! Brilliant! This will prove either his innocence or his guilt.'

'His innocence,' I stated. 'He was at home all day when the mother was murdered and he was also here when the son died.'

I was just pondering on who else the murderer might be, when Holmes interrupted my train of thought.

'This is obviously a very personal diary, judging by its contents,' reasoned Holmes. 'The ink has dried naturally, so is therefore a far darker blue than if blotting paper had been used. This means that the entries were all written on the day they happened. For instance, his entry for the 1st of May was written on the 1st of May. The father is obviously innocent. There is nothing more we can find out here, so let us go.'

We left the house as quietly as we had entered. Hailing a passing cab, we were soon speeding back towards Baker Street, where we warmed ourselves by a roaring fire in Holmes's apartment.

By the time the fire had died down, the time was quite late, so I headed home. Even though this case was so very mysterious, I was sure that the clouds were beginning to clear. I was confident that Holmes would wrap up this little mystery within a few days and expose the murderer. I was pleased that I had found the diary, solely because it proved the father's innocence.

The following day at my surgery was as dreary and as uneventful as usual. It was with great relief that I was eventually able to leave for Baker Street. Upon arriving in Holmes's apartment, I found him staring intently out of the window. I sidled up to the window beside him and glanced out. Mrs Wiggold was just descending from her carriage and was making her way towards the front of Holmes's house.

'It's Mrs Wiggold, Watson.'

'So I see.'

'Don't say a word, Watson, while she is present.'

'Quite so. I understand perfectly.'

'She must not even suppose that we know of her father's innocence. It will ruin all my plans if she does.'

A few moments later there was a sharp knock at the door and Mrs Wiggold entered. She hurried over to the fire, sat down in Holmes's chair and commenced rubbing her hands vigorously to induce some warmth in them.

'She is so much less shy than when she arrived two days ago. That's my chair she is sitting in as well. Oh, well, I suppose I must make sacrifices, all in the course of duty,' whispered Holmes to me under his breath.

He strode across to the fireplace and seated himself in an armchair.

'Mrs Wiggold,' began Holmes, 'I must ask you to come back in another two days, by which time I shall have fathomed this case. I must not detain you from visiting your husband in Lincolnshire any longer. Your train leaves in fifteen minutes.'

'How do you know that?' snapped Mrs Wiggold.

'Part of your train ticket is tucked into your glove and the destination is clearly visible, as is the time of the train's departure. Call back in two days, Mrs Wiggold. I shall have solved the case by then. You know where the door is.'

Mrs Wiggold left the room and from the window we watched her carriage speed away along Baker Street.

'Watson, do you fancy a trip to Lincolnshire?'

'Why, yes. I could do with a little break.'

'Come on then, let us go.'

A few minutes later our cab clattered under Euston Arch. Holmes pointed out Mrs Wiggold's carriage to me.

'It is evident that she has dismounted

from her carriage and is probably already on the train.'

'How can you tell?' I enquired cautiously, expecting a snappy answer.

'A brougham is mounted on elliptical springs. The springs will be compressed if someone is in the carriage. The springs on her carriage are not in the least compressed, therefore I conclude it is empty.' I shook my head in amazement at Holmes's powers of observation.

Holmes could see that I was dawdling. He grabbed my arm and we pushed our way through the crowds to the ticket office. After purchasing our tickets, we hurried on to platform 2 and boarded the train. We hurried to our designated coach and with real relief flung ourselves into our seats.

To my astonishment Holmes slipped me a wig under the table and told me to put it on in case Mrs Wiggold came past and recognized us.

'If she suspects she is being followed on this train, when we arrive in Lincoln, she will give us the slip by leading us all over Lincoln. She has an advantage over us because she knows the area. For two reasons I think she suspects she is being followed. The first is that she called at Baker Street a few minutes before her train would depart, making it almost impossible for us to board the same train. Secondly, she left her carriage in the forecourt of Euston Station knowing that I would see it and hoping I would assume she was inside it. This would prevent us from buying our tickets until the very last minute and diminish our chances of boarding the train,' explained Holmes.

The remainder of the journey passed uneventfully and after an hour we arrived at Lincoln. We followed Mrs Wiggold out of the station and our cab followed hers to her husband's address in Lincoln itself. We booked in at a hotel nearby and by six o'clock next morning we were watching the house.

After half an hour of fruitless watching, Holmes remarked, 'This murderer is clever. I studied the deaths column in the *Times* this morning to see if Mrs Wiggold's brother was killed yesterday. He was not. This could mean that he is the murderer. I think Mrs Wiggold is innocent, namely because if she had killed her brother, she would be in some state of distress. She was perfectly calm when she called at Baker Street yesterday morning and she had plenty of colour in her face. All murderers lose the colour in their cheeks for a minimum of twelve hours after a murder they have committed. In view of this, she is therefore innocent.'

A few minutes later Mrs Wiggold hurried out of her house and made her way towards the station. Five minutes later a man we assumed was her husband left the house and sauntered after her. We waited for five minutes then, with the aid of Holmes's master key, we slipped inside their house. It was a dark, dingy and rather pokey house. We made our way into the sitting room and Holmes crossed over to the desk in the far corner which overlooked the garden. He began reading the manuscript which lay on the desk.

'How deplorable,' he began after a few minutes reading. 'There's no plot to this story and no action. There is an apostrophe missed here and there's a split infinitive!' he exploded, pointing wildly at a page. He hurled the manuscript onto the desk. 'It is a grammatical graveyard!' he exploded once more. 'I'll bet any sum of money, Watson, that his books are not reprinted a dozen or so times. While I search the drawers on the right-hand side of the desk, you search those on the left.'

The last drawer Holmes came to had a sturdy padlock on it.

'My master key will soon resolve the matter,' he chuckled as he felt in his pocket for the key.

Once the drawer was opened, Holmes's nimble fingers darted among its contents. There was a small glass bottle, a few receipts, some maps of London and a blue stiffly covered book with the word 'Diary' embossed on the front cover. Holmes snatched it up and flipped through its pages. Eventually he found what he was searching for. It was the entry for the day Mrs Wiggold's mother died. It ran as follows: 'Mother-in-law died.' The entry for two days before was considerably more interesting. 'Got up early. Went to London on the 7.15. Visited mother-in-law. Administered the amount required for it to take effect in two days. Will stay at home tomorrow and all the day after to avert suspicion.'

'This case is becoming less bewildering than it was at first,' remarked Holmes. He handed the diary to me, then picked up the empty glass bottle. I glanced quickly at several of the entries in the diary, then began to read the label on the glass bottle. The letters were in block capitals and written in black ink so they were clearly legible. They read as follows: 'The liquid in this bottle contains 14 parts water to 1 part poison from the Poison Arrow Frog. Half of the contents of the bottle will kill a healthy adult in two days. This is a very rarely known poison. It has been watered down so that it will not show up in any poison test. It is important to note that 48 hours after having been drunk, the poison will kill. The person who drank it will die within seconds once it takes effect.'

'It is rather badly written,' remarked Holmes as he put the diary and the bottle back into the drawer and locked it. We then left the house and hurried to the station, where we boarded the next train and were soon back in London. During the journey, Holmes explained the case a little more to me.

'The drawer containing the bottle and the diary was locked for one reason: so that his wife could not open it. The reason that the eldest brother was found floating in the river is simple. On his way to work he had to pass over Westminster Bridge and he paused to lean on the side and stare at the flowing river. The poison struck while he was doing so and he fell in. Owing to the fact that his lungs were full of water, he was pronounced drowned.

'The husband has a bottle of the frog poison in his possession, which he will administer to the other brother some time today. It is our duty to endeavour to stop him doing so before it is too late!'

'Holmes, I have two questions to ask you.'

'Ask them and they shall be answered.'

'How do you know for sure that the husband has a bottle of the poison in his possession and what is the Poison Arrow Frog?'

'I found the receipt that came with the poison. It clearly stated that there were two bottles of poison. There was only one bottle in the desk, so the other must be in his possession. In answer to your question about the frog, it is red and black and lives in the jungles of South America. The Indians there use its poison for the tips of their arrows when hunting. Despite its being so very small, it is the most venomous creature on earth.'

A little later our train pulled into Euston Station. We hurried to the exit and were soon on a hansom trundling to Baker Street. Upon arrival in Holmes's apartment, we had a light snack and then hurried to the Bank of England.

During the journey, Holmes explained how he knew that Mrs Wiggold's brother was employed there.

'While we were searching Mrs Wiggold's house, I found her address book. It gave her brother's residential address and his work address. We are heading to the Bank at the moment in the hope that I shall be in time to urge him not to drink anything at all today.'

The instant we arrived at the Bank Holmes darted up the steps and burst inside. Ordering a constable inside to follow him, Holmes hurried down a long corridor, then paused momentarily outside a panelled pine door, before suddenly slipping inside.

Mrs Wiggold's brother was facing the window and pouring some port wine into a glass. Meanwhile Mrs Wiggold's husband was pouring the contents of a small glass bottle into her brother's cup of tea. It was evident that even with my rather primitive observational skills, I could see at once what had taken place. The brother was granting his brother-in-law an interview. The latter had asked for a glass of port and while his unsuspecting brother-in-law was away from his desk pouring the port, the husband had poured the poison into his brother-in-law's cup of tea in the hope that he would return to finish it off. We had burst in upon the scene just as the poison was being poured into the tea.

'Aha!' shouted Holmes, 'Caught you red-handed!' snatching the bottle of poison from the husband and handing it to Mrs Wiggold's brother. 'Do you see now why we had to interrupt this interview, James?' Holmes enquired, staring at him as he spoke.

'Indeed I do, Mr Holmes. But how do you know my first name?'

'It is written in Gothic script upon the name plate on your door.'

At this point Mrs Wiggold's husband spoke.

'I do not intend to make a dramatic scene at this point. I am fully aware that my fate is sealed.' He seized the cup containing the tea and gulped it down. 'Holmes and myself are fully aware that in two days I shall be dead. During my brief stay in prison I do not wish to receive any hospitality or kindness. I am aware of the great financial strain on the prison service and do not wish to make that strain any greater.'

After his brief announcement he was handcuffed by the constable who had followed Holmes and was then led out of the room. James thanked Holmes very heartily for having saved his life and that of his sister. Holmes headed for Baker Street and I traced my way home to chronicle this adventure of ours.

To save Mrs Wiggold any unnecessary distress, Holmes informed her that the murderer had drowned at sea. Mrs Wiggold ceased to suspect her father and her husband died in prison two days after his arrest.

A Case for the Admiralty

It was a warm summer evening as I made my way up to Holmes's apartment. Upon opening the door, I discovered Holmes to be in deep conversation with a tall, fair gentleman sporting a cravat and tail coat. Without turning round, Holmes heartily welcomed me.

'You have your back to me!' I exclaimed. 'How did you know it was I and not a client?'

'In the first place, my dear Watson, you did not knock before you came in. If it had been a client ascending the staircase, there would have been a slight pause on reaching the landing, before that person summoned the temerity to knock. Your tread upon the stairs was distinctly male. A female would tread much more lightly. I hope that answers your question, Watson. Please take a seat and make yourself at home.'

Holmes eased himself into an armchair

and offered the tall gentleman a seat. This offer was declined.

'Will you please proceed, Mr Barton?' enquired Holmes.

'As I was saying,' began Mr Barton, 'we cannot overestimate the seriousness of this problem. I have no wish to alarm you, Mr Holmes, but you have three days to save the nation. Goodbye.'

'Goodbye,' replied Holmes, chuckling, for such a challenge is irresistible to him. 'Well, my dear Watson, I suppose you have a right to know what this case is about. Mr Barton is from the Admiralty. He was telling me that some documents and a series of blueprints have gone missing. They described and illustrated in great detail the concept and design of the world's first turbine-powered battleship. Four days ago the Admiralty received this typewritten letter,' explained Holmes, handing it to me. 'As you can see, it demands five million pounds in cash, or he will sell these secrets to the Germans. This would be a disaster for Britain. Think of the Naval Race.'

'Why, yes!' I exclaimed. 'This would

put Germany one step ahead of us.'

Holmes snatched the letter back and began to examine it.

'He's not as clever as he thinks he is.'

'How do you know it's a man?'

'If it were a woman, the letter would not be so very clearly marked. He is also left-handed.'

'How can you tell that from a typewritten letter?'

Holmes showed me the keyboard of his typewriter and with his index finger divided the keys into two groups for me.

'All of the letters that would be typed by the left hand are more distinct than those by the right hand. He is stronger in his left hand, so that I must conclude he is left-handed. It's not as simple as that though, Watson. He has tried to confuse us.'

'How?' I enquired.

'By a very simple trick. The letter 'a' should be typed by the little and weakest finger of the left hand; he has typed it with the right. The letter 'h' should be typed with the right hand; he has typed it with the left. I can tell this because all the 'a's' are more distinct than they should be and all the 'h's' are less distinct than they should be. As you see there is always an explanation. He is also missing his right index finger. There are no letters typed with the right index finger, so it has to be missing. This chap is clever but not quite clever enough to fool me. Call again tomorrow, Watson, at about four in the afternoon and bring your revolver with you. We may need it. I have my trap to lay and I will need some bait. There is nothing more we can do tonight. Goodnight, Watson.'

'Goodnight. And the best of luck for the case — '

'Thank you, Watson, but I do not require any luck,' interrupted Holmes. 'You are creating a draught. Please close the door from the outside.'

I did as he requested and left Baker Street. As I sauntered home I was confident that Holmes knew exactly who the villain was, otherwise he would not have asked me to bring my revolver with me to our next meeting. I had no suspicions that he intended to commit suicide just because he could not solve this case. The only clue as to the identity of the letter writer was the fact that he was left-handed. This gave us very little to go on. I regretted walking all the way home in the warmth of a summer evening because when I arrived I was absolutely exhausted. I went straight to bed and to slip between the cool sheets was incomparable joy.

The following afternoon I arrived at Baker Street exactly at four o'clock. I found Holmes slouching in his favourite armchair, his pipe hanging somewhat precariously from his mouth and with his eyes scarcely open.

'Ah, Watson!' he exclaimed, waving his pipe about, an action which threw ash all over the carpet. I was pointed to a chair and quickly obeyed his instruction.

'We have precious little time, Watson. In view of the recent crisis the PM has requested my presence at Downing Street as soon as possible. Because you are my chronicler, I have made arrangements for you to accompany me.'

'I am most grateful,' I replied.

'By now,' continued Holmes, glancing up at the clock upon the mantelpiece, 'there will be a carriage waiting outside which will convey us with, I presume, all possible speed to Downing Street.'

Five minutes later, our brougham turned right into Downing Street. I had never imagined in my whole existence that I should ever cross the portals of number 10 Downing Street. The entrance lobby was designed in the late Regency style with grand fireplaces and a huge, sweeping staircase that led up to the Cabinet Room. A civil servant showed us up to it.

'I'm afraid the Prime Minister is in the process of reading a brief, twelve-thousand-page report about the Naval Race,' we were informed drily by a senior civil servant.

We were shown into the Cabinet Room. It was a spacious and airy room with large chandeliers hanging from the high ceiling. The Prime Minister sat facing us, with his face buried in a massive Civil Service report. Behind him was a plain Regency marble fireplace. We seated ourselves on two of the many chairs that were arranged along the sides of the boat-shaped table. We waited for the Prime Minister to acknowledge our presence. After a few minutes, Holmes coughed twice, in the vain hope of attracting the Prime Minister's attention. There was no response.

Talking to the Prime Minister was like talking to a wax doll that should have been wrapped up and put away many years ago. Holmes coughed again. There was still no response.

Holmes clapped his hands and leaned forward. He murmured, 'Prime Minister, there has been an earthquake in Tunbridge Wells!'

'Good,' murmured the Prime Minister in response, not even glancing up from the report he was reading.

'Prime Minister, the Germans are marching up Whitehall!'

'Good.'

Holmes sighed and leaned back in his chair.

'Well, well,' he remarked, more to himself than to anyone else, 'I am aware of the fact that most politicians are inert, but I had no idea they all would be so!'

I nodded in reply to his statement.

Holmes leaned forward and began again.

'Prime Minister, there is a by-election tomorrow in a marginal constituency.'

'What!' roared the Prime Minister, looking up from the report and staring at Holmes with fiery, bloodshot eyes. His hands were trembling a little and he was panting.

'A by-election! In a . . . what . . . er . . . how . . . why?'

'Calm down, Prime Minister,' interrupted Holmes. 'I had no other choice. I wanted your undivided attention because I have no wish to be here till next Wednesday.'

'You *had* my undivided attention.'

'Undivided?' questioned Holmes. 'More like shredded.'

'Well, now that you have my attention, perhaps you will tell me what you want?'

'What *I* want?' bellowed Holmes.

'Oh, yes, of course,' replied the Prime Minister. 'Now, I summoned you here on a matter of some importance. These secrets are vital to Britain and it is essential that you retrieve them.'

'Well, I'll try, Prime Minister,' replied Holmes.

We both sauntered out of Downing Street and made our way to Baker Street.

Some time later we were lounging in Holmes's armchairs in front of a blazing fire. After I had consumed a few glasses of brandy, Holmes raised his chin from his chest and remarked, 'The person who stole these plans must have worked for the Admiralty.'

'How do you deduce that?' I enquired.

'For two reasons. Firstly, to be near the plans, he must work in the Admiralty. Secondly, to know of their existence and their extreme value and importance, proves my point that he must have worked for the Admiralty.'

'What do you mean, worked?'

'He intends to get his revenge on the Admiralty. He was recently sacked. This is why he stole the documents in the first place. As a sort of punishment for the Admiralty. It may interest you to know,

Watson, that Mr Barton compiled this list for me from his knowledge of recent dismissals at the Admiralty.'

He handed me a piece of paper which was folded over about a dozen times. I began to unfold it.

'You will find five names and addresses on that paper, Watson, They are the five remaining suspects.'

'How do you know they are the remaining suspects?'

'Oh really, Watson,' Holmes growled. 'These five are the only people who were sacked this year. People who were sacked last year have to be innocent, because the turbine became common knowledge this year. Anybody who was sacked this year is therefore a suspect. I asked Mr Barton, who was good enough to give me the list, if any of the people mentioned happened to be left-handed. Watson, I'd like you to look at the last name on the list. It is most interesting.'

I did as he asked and read the name and address a few times over to myself. I was aware that my deductive powers were somewhat weak, but I failed to see how this name and address could be so interesting to my friend.

'Why this name and address?' I enquired.

'Out of all the names on this list, he is the only one who is left-handed. Seeing that the ransom note was typed by someone who was left-handed, this naturally aroused my suspicions. I headed straight for his address, only to discover something which aroused my suspicions even more. When I arrived in the street in which he was supposed to live, Elias Place, I was shocked and amazed to see that there was no number 36, which was where my list stated that he lived, as there were only thirty houses in the street. Consequently, I returned to Baker Street. I had been deceived, Watson, by an amateur! I hung my head in shame for the rest of the morning,' he chuckled to himself.

'Oh, don't worry, Holmes. He may not have been an amateur,' I said.

'He is!' answered Holmes. 'The fact that he sent a note to the Admiralty, informing them of what he has done, is completely amateurish.'

'He must be a very clever amateur to have eluded and confused you,' I replied. 'Please pardon my ignorance, Holmes — '

'Very well then, Watson, I will make this exception.'

After being interrupted so brusquely by Holmes, I paused for a moment to collect my thoughts, then asked the question that I would have asked had I not been interrupted.

'Holmes, how can you be sure he lives south of the river?'

'The postmark on the envelope that contained the ransom note indicated that it had been posted in SE11, which is south of the river. He wishes to elude the police for as long as possible, so will create a false impression that the thief lives in south-east London, whereas our suspect resides in south-west London which would appear to be many miles away from the postmark. But I have ascertained that there is a spot in Vauxhall where SW8 sits cheek by jowl with SE11. One need take only fifteen paces from Elias Place, SW8, to arrive in Hanover

Gardens, SE11. All he has had to do is to go fifteen paces out of his house to arrive in south-east London. Now do you understand, Watson?'

'Yes. And thank you for your explanation. I do begin to understand your powers of reasoning a little more.'

'Watson, seeing that time is not on our side, I suggest that we take a cab to south London instantly. Are you agreeable to my proposal?'

'Oh, very much so. I have no complaints whatsoever.'

Our cab took us to Elias Place. By the time we had arrived it was dark. The stars shone brightly in the sky, like fragments of glass reflecting a shining light. Holmes strode up the street towards number 30, with myself in hot pursuit.

When we arrived outside, which as Holmes had stated, was the very last house in the street, he motioned for me to be silent. Across the street from us was a man leaning against a fence smoking a cigarette. He turned and made his way down the alley that connected Elias Place with a neighbouring street. We followed him silently. Upon reaching the end of the alley, we squatted down behind a small tree that had sprung up between the cobbles of the alley and in the dimly lit street we could faintly make out the figure of the man we had seen earlier. He went into a house that was shrouded in darkness. We heard the faint sound of the front door closing.

'Number 23,' whispered Holmes to me.

'How can you tell?' I enquired. 'I cannot see the number.'

'There is no number visible. His house is between numbers 21 and 25, so by the simple process of deduction it must be 23. Elementary, my dear Watson. And now,' he whispered, even softer than before, 'we must proceed to south-east London.'

I followed with neither sound nor word. We returned back along the alley we had previously come through, then turned left into Elias Place. When we reached the end of the street, we turned left and after a few yards, we were at the far end of Hanover Gardens.

After a few minutes, we heard the

sound of a door opening and then closing. We saw our suspect slink towards the opposite street. Holmes instructed me to follow, then melted silently away. A few minutes later he returned.

'He is back where we saw him last, leaning against the fence,' he whispered softly. 'Come on, Watson. We must hurry.'

We slipped stealthily out of our hiding place and made our way towards number 23. We hurried up the garden path, endeavouring as much as possible not to trip over on the uneven flagstones. Eventually we reached the front door. It looked dilapidated, with flaking paint peeling off it and the door knocker at an angle, clinging perilously to the door by one rusty nail. Holmes grasped my arm and we hurried into a corner of the front garden that contained a few shrubs.

We squatted down on the damp earth and Holmes began to explain his plan to me. I feel it is only fair to point out to the reader that my hearing is particularly acute. However, I still had to strain myself and listen most intently to Holmes's whispered plan, if I was to comprehend it or to carry out his instructions. The parts of the plan that I could make out ran as follows: we would sit noiselessly in the garden until the suspect arrived. We could not move an inch until the suspect had gone into the house. When a light came on in a room, Holmes would creep to the window and peer in. He assured me that the first thing the man would check upon would be the stolen plans, seeing that they were his most valuable possessions. That was why Holmes would creep over to the window, in order to see where they were hidden. Once Holmes had discovered the place in question, we were to wait in hiding until the suspect left the house again and headed to the opposite street. We would then break into the house as quietly as possible and head for their place of concealment. Once we had gathered up the plans, we would head back to Baker Street with all possible speed.

The instant Holmes finished relating the plan, he motioned me to be silent and still. I froze instantly. A minute or two later, the suspect sidled up the garden path. He turned sharply to see if he was being observed or followed. After satisfying himself, he slowly turned back round again. He undid three or four sturdy locks, then entered his abode. The cacophony which followed was one I do not expect ever to hear again. It was evident that on the other side of the door, he possessed a good two dozen bolts which he was securing with great rapidity.

Holmes laughed to himself.

'Not expecting many guests tonight, is he?' Holmes whispered. He then hurried over to the window. The light in the front room was turned on, Holmes craned his long neck to see in through a tear in one of the curtains. He suddenly ducked down below the window sill and remained there motionless. A shadow loomed up behind the curtains, which were then flung open. I was petrified. Even though I was behind a shrub which covered me perfectly, I had some nagging suspicion that all was not well. Eventually the curtains were re-drawn and he withdrew. Soon the sound of the many bolts being withdrawn was audible. The suspect relocked the door from the outside and hurried off back to Elias Place.

Once he had gone, Holmes crossed over to the door. He put his shoulder against it but it would not budge. It looked rickety and unstable but it held firm and would not give way. Holmes produced his skeleton key and we were soon inside the house. It was pitch dark. The house smelt of damp. Holmes struck a match. By its flickering light we saw only the dismal sight of peeling wallpaper, flaking paint and loose floorboards. We made our way into the front room, where Holmes struck another match. We dared not use any more powerful method of lighting in case it was visible from the street.

The front room was quite small, with double doors at one end, which led through to the back room which was used, as far as I could gather, as a general storeroom. Whilst I was exploring the front room and the adjoining room with the light of a match Holmes had given me, he was busy feeling either side of a small gold-framed picture. His left hand was fluttering up and down the left-hand side of the picture. His right hand gently pulled at the right-hand side of the picture. To my amazement, the picture rotated to reveal a square alcove which contained a safe.

The match burnt out. Another was lit. Holmes rotated the different combinations of the lock and the safe opened.

'How did you know what the combination was?' I enquired, rather stunned that my friend had opened it with such ease.

'There is a perfectly simple mathematical method for working out the combination of every safe in the world,' replied Holmes. 'An old friend of mine who has worked with safes for over twenty years told me the method. There are only two things required to work it out. Firstly, the type and number of the safe, which are printed on the door; secondly, the ability to calculate in your head the most complex equation ever conceived. It is only this gentleman and myself who are acquainted with this method, so I am afraid, Watson, that I cannot confide it even to you. Your chronicle of this adventure will have to be without it.'

While Holmes was speaking his hands were fiddling about in the safe in the hope of finding something of value to this case. He brought out a large leather wallet, full of papers and a very large piece of paper that had been rolled up. Holmes put these under his arm and strode out of the house. I followed close behind him. It was not long before we were on our way back to Baker Street in the comfort of a cab.

'Holmes?'

'Yes, Watson?'

'How do you know that the wallet of documents under your arm and the roll of paper are the plans that you have been entrusted to recover and take back to the Admiralty?'

Holmes lit his pipe and puffed away like a steam train.

'It is simple. In such a rundown house the only documents that could have been of any value to him are the stolen ones.'

'Quite so, I understand now.'

Presently, we were back in Baker Street fully appreciating the benefits of a glowing fire.

'I wish to ascertain,' remarked Holmes,

'whether or not these are the plans the Admiralty have commissioned me to retrieve for them. If, when an official from the Admiralty calls, and they turn out to be other documents of considerably less value, then I shall be the laughing stock of Scotland Yard for many years to come.'

'Everyone makes mistakes,' I interjected, endeavouring, as best as possible, to reassure him.

'Precisely, Doctor. Even Homer nodded.'

I could not help feeling that the comparison between himself and Homer was not completely unfounded. There was always a firm foundation for each of his answers, even this one.

Holmes took up the wallet of documents and began sifting through them. A few moments later, he slammed it shut.

'I am content. Those are the documents I was searching for. I shouldn't doubt myself so much, Watson; bad for my self-esteem, you know.'

'Holmes, I do not wish you to think me a complete idiot, but how did you know the man that we saw in Elias Place, smoking a cigarette, was your suspect and not just an innocent person who happened to be there at the time?'

'Well, in answer to your question, Watson, the person had to be our suspect for a number of reasons. To begin with, he held his cigarette in his left hand so must have been left-handed. He also was missing his right index finger, which I had already deduced from his typewritten letter. These observations have turned the finger of guilt in the correct direction. I was still not wholly convinced. Lastly, in view of the fact that he is an amateur, I was sure that if I was ever to see him, it would be in Elias Place. A typical amateur would visit the false address that he had given, or be as close to it as humanly possible, in order to discover if the police were following him yet. If the police were on his tail, they would be most likely to head straight to Elias Place, not of course realizing that number 36 did not exist. Once he had seen the police searching Elias Place in vain for him, he would be aware of his impending danger and take whatever measures he thought necessary to avoid imprisonment. I was convinced that he was the man we were searching for, when he led us to his house. The number of bolts and locks he had on the door proved that I was correct, as always, Watson.'

We both stared mutely into the fire, both of us expecting the other to start a conversation. There was silence, apart from the ticking of the clock and the occasional crackling of the logs on the fire. The monotony of these sounds was momentarily broken by the clatter of a carriage in Baker Street. There was a patter of feet upon the stairs. The door was flung open and in stormed Mr Barton.

'Oh, do come in, Mr Barton,' remarked Holmes, still staring mutely into the fire.

'Holmes!' bellowed Mr Barton, 'I thought you were a detective!'

Holmes frowned.

'I am.'

'I thought you could unravel mysteries and solve crimes!'

Holmes frowned again.

'I can and I do.'

'Well, you have failed to do so in this case!'

Holmes knitted his brows and glared at Mr Barton.

'What do you mean?' he enquired.

'I mean that you have failed to recover any — '

'Oh, do sit down, Mr Barton,' interrupted Holmes. 'I am afraid that you are rather wearing out the carpet, with your incessant pacing of the room. Sit down!'

Mr Barton obeyed his instruction.

Holmes sat on the edge of his chair and began.

'Mr Barton, you came to me a few days ago in a state of some distress. You begged and implored me to recover plans of vital importance. They related to the turbine.'

At this point Holmes leaned back in his chair, snatched up the wallet of documents and tossed it into Mr Barton's lap. He did exactly the same with the roll of paper that had come with the wallet of documents.

Mr Barton was speechless. His mouth dropped open.

'I am most grateful,' he stammered. 'Britain, the Empire and, most importantly, the Admiralty will be eternally grateful to you for this monumental service you have done us. We owe you a gargantuan debt of gratitude. Britain's security is no longer threatened, thanks to you, Holmes. Britannia will rule the waves for generations to come!'

'Well, don't stop there, Mr Barton. Pray continue. Do not hesitate to praise me to the skies again, should you feel thus inclined. Mr Barton, owing to your incessant fidgeting, I must ask you to leave. You may go.'

'Goodbye, Holmes.'

Mr Barton paused in the doorway. He clutched the plans close to his chest and implored, 'I never doubted you, Holmes, I never doubted you for a single minute.' He unintentionally slammed the door and hurried downstairs.

'Well, well,' chuckled Holmes. 'This case, although stressful, has not been without its highlights. I have, however, learnt only two things from this case. Firstly, I am more than a match for any criminal; secondly, I always give far too generously to cab drivers!'

The Three-faced Villain

Holmes was smoking his pipe in front of a roaring coal fire and I was extinguishing my fifth cigar into a somewhat congested ashtray, when Holmes sat up in his chair.

'Hush, Watson.'

I was barely making any noise with my cigar, but I obeyed his instruction. Presently I heard some faint footsteps on the staircase. These gradually became audible as the visitor came closer.

'It is a lady,' remarked Holmes, 'with small feet and about thirty-five years old.'

'It's amazing that you can tell all that from footsteps,' I marvelled.

'I quite agree, but all my methods of deduction are extremely simple, Watson. People understand them once they have been explained. For instance, the person ascending the staircase is a lady because the footfalls are light. The lady has small feet, because her footfall is faint. A lady's age is rarely mentioned in polite society for obvious reasons. Discovering a lady's age before you have even seen her is quite a skill and takes years of practice to accomplish. I deduced this lady's age by the time lapse between each footfall. The footfalls that we are dealing with here have a very short time lapse between each one, so the lady will be quite young. I assumed her age to be about thirty-five.'

'Well, Holmes, let us see if your deductions are correct,' I remarked.

'Yes, Watson, let us do that. I have never awaited the arrival of a client as eagerly as this before. Not even when I first started detecting and was desperate for any client to whom I could be of service.'

Presently the footsteps ceased and there was a faint knock at the door.

'Come in!'

A small lady peered round the door, then entered the room cautiously.

'Would you, by any chance, be Mr Sherlock Holmes?'

'No, madam, I am not.' I gasped at this point. I felt quite ashamed of Holmes lying to an innocent lady. 'I am not *Mr*

Sherlock Holmes,' said he. 'I am the *great* Sherlock Holmes.'

The lady looked somewhat taken aback at Holmes's arrogance. However, when Holmes vacated his armchair for her, then asked her if she would care to sit, she smiled and I am convinced that it was at this point that she began to feel more at home and less afraid of Holmes.

Holmes stood in front of the fire, with his hands deep in his trouser pockets and his pipe thrust firmly between his thin, parched lips.

'Madam,' he began. 'I hope and believe that you have not arrived here solely to rest your tired feet and to shelter from the rain. I assume that your presence here indicates that you have a case for us to solve.'

'Quite right, Mr Holmes,' answered our client.

'Pray relate the facts to us in the exact order that they occurred. Then I shall solve your case for you. In order to conserve as much time as possible, please limit the duration of them by as much as possible. Please, no sudden outbursts of anxiety, they merely reduce the length of my already short temper.'

I pulled my chair slightly closer, so as not to miss any fact that might be mumbled or muttered for reasons of extreme delicacy.

'Before you begin, madam, perhaps you would care to enlighten us as to your name and present place of residence,' enquired Holmes.

'Certainly. My name is Mrs Hurst and at present I reside at number 51, Cadogan Place.'

Holmes's eyebrows rose.

'Not *the* Cadogan Place?' he enquired.

'Yes, Mr Holmes, the Cadogan Place, near Sloane Square. Why? Is something the matter with my address, Mr Holmes?' enquired our client.

'Well, madam, to be able to live in Cadogan Place, either you or your husband must be extremely well provided for,' remarked Holmes.

'My husband is the richest member of our family. We were practically a penniless couple when we married. My husband became an employee in a large bank in the City. Rung by rung he climbed the ladder of success and with tremendous rapidity. Within seven years he became manager of the bank. I never expected we would become rich, let alone that our ascendancy would proceed at the speed it did. I originally married my husband for love and looks, not for money. He married me for love.'

At this juncture I realized that Mrs Hurst was unnecessarily shy and extremely modest about her good looks. If I was asked to describe Mrs Hurst I would say that her nose was a little too short, her mouth just a little too wide and her hair was somewhat too wavy. She appeared to be an amazing combination of imperfections, but hers was a complexion and a beauty that men could see in their dreams without the least feeling of shame.

'Pray continue, Mrs Hurst,' ordered Holmes.

'I came here, Mr Holmes, to tell you about a shocking state of affairs in London cabs. A fortnight ago I decided to have afternoon tea in Harrods, which, as I am sure you already know, is a mere six or seven hundred yards away from Cadogan Place.'

'I was aware of that, Mrs Hurst,' answered Holmes. 'You should have no need to stop again during your explanation of your difficulties with London cab drivers.'

'I hailed a hansom cab and instructed the driver to drive to Harrods. I remember he had a beard and kept one hand over part of his face. Also, he did not speak a word, just nodded his head. When we arrived outside Harrods, I expected that the fare would be very little more than a shilling in view of the short distance we had travelled. The driver grunted out that the fare was three guineas. I was astounded and shocked that it was such a vast sum. I made a little fuss, but eventually paid. As you know, Mr Holmes, one cannot dismount from a hansom cab until the driver opens the doors. He would not open the doors until I had paid him. If I wanted to be released, which I did, I would have to pay this unfair sum. That was why I paid him. I had no alternative.

'Whilst I was taking tea in Harrods, I resolved never again to ride in a cab driven by a bearded driver for fear of being robbed again. I was determined never to allow this disagreeable incident to occur again. A few days later, I was in South Kensington after visiting a friend's house. I was quite tired and felt I would not be able to return home on foot. It began to rain and the downpour was the deciding factor in my decision to take a cab home. My desperation was not great enough for me to accept a bearded driver, but just then a moustached driver came along with his hansom cab. He appeared to have something in his left eye, judging by the ferocity with which he was rubbing it. It was only afterwards I realized it was a cunning ruse for hiding part of his face from me. At the time I had not the least suspicion of this clean-shaven driver with a bushy moustache and evidently something in his eye. He drove me from the Boltons to Cadogan Place. Upon arrival at my address, I was asked for ten guineas. I naturally refused to pay such an extravagant sum but realized after making this foolish statement that he held the upper hand. I was his captive, at his mercy. Eventually I gave in, paid him and was released.

'I began to suspect that London cab drivers were a band of criminals who were ready to pounce on unsuspecting travellers. I vowed to refuse to board any cab if the driver was bearded or had a moustache. This would naturally limit me somewhat as to the cabs I could take, but the great distress the two earlier incidents had caused me compelled me to take that action. I felt sure that now there would be no recurrence.

'Some time after this second unhappy incident, I was strolling back to Cadogan Place from Green Park. As I was passing Hyde Park Corner, the heat began to intensify and by the time I had arrived in Belgrave Square, it had become intolerable. I was plodding slowly on, almost completely drained of energy. Every step was becoming an increasing strain, the perspiration was making me very uncomfortable. I was on the point of collapsing when a cab drove up. It took my very last ounce of energy to hail it. I staggered aboard, after contenting myself that the cab driver had neither beard nor moustache. The only strange thing about him was that he was tweaking his nose most ferociously. Naturally that did not seem in the least suspicious to me at the time. I was, however, soon to learn otherwise. It was a mere half a mile to my house at the most. I was charged the extortionate fare of two guineas. I begrudgingly paid, seeing that I had no other alternative.'

'What do you wish me to do, Mrs Hurst?' enquired Holmes.

'I would like, if it is possible, for you to find out who these three people are, and why they overcharged me so very much. Is it a general problem in London or are these three men targeting me in particular?'

'Very well, Mrs Hurst,' was the only reply.

'Do you think that these three people who overcharged me are members of a gang or organization?'

'No. You were not overcharged by three people. It was the same person in each instance.'

'How could that be, Mr Holmes, when one driver was bearded, the other had a moustache and the last one was cleanly shaven?'

'Mrs Hurst, I am aware of the fact that you are a woman but have you never heard of the safety razor?' asked Holmes.

'Why, yes. My husband uses it frequently, but I fail to see what that has to do with this case.'

'It is elementary, Mrs Hurst,' insisted Holmes. 'This driver needed only to shave off his beard in order to confuse you. He would leave his moustache, of course. That would be his next disguise. After you had paid his extortionate demand, he would shave off his moustache to prevent you recognizing him next time. Then he would overcharge you again. This time he would be clean-shaven to create the impression that it was not the same person each time. What I need to know from you now, Mrs Hurst, is if you have dismissed any servants recently.'

'Well, yes and no. My husband dismissed our butler three weeks ago on grounds of impertinence, for he had found him in the music room looking through my sheet music.'

'Very strange!'

'I persuaded my husband to overlook the offence and reinstate the man later the same day, because he is such a competent servant who has been with us since we were married.'

'Does this partially dismissed butler have any outstanding facial features which would make him instantly recognizable? A large scar running down his face, for instance?'

'No, definitely no large scar on his face.'

'Very well, Mrs Hurst, take a cab back to your residence in Cadogan Place, but make sure the driver is not bearded. Watson and myself will follow presently.'

Mrs Hurst rose reluctantly, it seemed to me, and left the warmth of the apartment.

'This cab driver, and I use the term advisedly, has a large and distinctive scar on the left side of his face. Also, this scar stretches the whole length of his face.'

'Can you really be so certain of that, Holmes?' I enquired.

'Oh, yes, Watson. The fact that he grew a beard, then still had to cover his face from her, suggests a very large scar that even a beard would be insufficient to conceal. The fact that every time she encountered this cab driver, his hand covered the whole length of the left side of his face confirms my suspicions that he has such a scar.'

'Would not this man simply wish to hide himself from possible identification? Do you have any suspicions as to who it might be?'

'As yet, Watson, no. Though I have every hope that this case will become yet another one of my many successes. We must not waste another moment, Watson. Let us proceed to 51 Cadogan Place.'

We left the cosy apartment behind and presently passed Hyde Park Corner and St George's Hospital. Soon our cab drew up outside 51 Cadogan Place and it was in a far grander area of London than I had expected. Cadogan Place is a large, lengthy terrace of white stuccoed houses.

Each property had its own covered balcony on the first floor, and grand pediments adorned each window of the house. Whilst Holmes rang the door bell, I continued to marvel at the grandeur of the terrace and remarked to Holmes how very imposing the houses all were.

'Quite so, Watson. These houses are far more ornate than the rather plain ones in Baker Street.'

No sooner had Holmes made this remark than the door was opened by Mrs Hurst's butler. Holmes and I entered, not too sure what to expect from such a valued individual.

'You are expected, sir,' stated the butler in perfectly polite tones. Then, turning in my direction, he enquired, 'May I take your hat, sir?' I declined this offer as politely as I possibly could. The butler swivelled round and asked Holmes the same question he had asked me.

'I am perfectly capable,' snapped Holmes, 'to be the guardian of my own headgear.'

This rude rebuttal shocked the butler greatly.

'Mrs Hurst is in the morning room,' he said much more stiffly than when he had first addressed us. 'I shall take you to her. Please follow me.'

He paced off, with us following leisurely behind him. We were shown into an upstairs room where Mrs Hurst was sitting on a sofa reading a large leather-bound book.

'Ah, Smithson,' she remarked upon our entry into the room, 'you may leave us now. Bring some tea in five minutes.'

Bowing slightly on receiving these instructions, the butler glided out of the room.

'Homer?' enquired Holmes, glancing at the book in Mrs Hurst's hands.

'Quite correct, Mr Holmes. In the original Greek as well.'

'Recreational reading?' asked Holmes, with a twinkle in his eye.

Mrs Hurst smiled at Holmes's little joke.

'I am happy to inform you, Mrs Hurst, that I am much closer to discovering the culprit's identity than I was before I saw your butler,' explained Holmes.

'How could your seeing my butler help you?' enquired Mrs Hurst.

'We are aware that the cab driver, if he is a cab driver, has some mark on the left side of his face. Most probably a scar or a birthmark of sorts, which would make him easily identifiable. Your butler has a birthmark on his chin. I am, therefore, left no choice but to suspect him of the crimes committed against you. Notice that I used the word 'suspect' for I am not wholly convinced of his involvement.'

'But, Mr Holmes, if your suspect has some mark of sorts and my butler has such a mark, that is surely cast-iron evidence that proves his guilt? Though I would be most sorry to find that the case.'

'No. It is more like modelling-clay evidence. The suspect I am searching for has a mark stretching down the whole side of his face. Your butler has merely a small birthmark an inch or so along his chin.'

'So what does his birthmark prove?'

'Nothing as such. It only means that there is a very slim chance that he is our suspect.'

'But the — '

'Hush,' interrupted Holmes.

A few moments later I heard the faint footfall of the butler ascending the stairs with the tea he had been ordered to bring up five minutes before.

We waited in silence as the footsteps grew closer and louder. Eventually the door was opened and the butler appeared, clutching a large tray with tea for three and a considerable assortment of cakes. The butler placed the tray on the coffee table. Mrs Hurst dismissed him from the room. We waited until his footsteps had died away, then Holmes broke the silence.

'On each occasion you saw our suspect, was the whole of the left side of his face covered by his hand?'

'Yes.'

'Then this mark on his face must occupy a far larger area and length than that of the small birthmark of your butler.' Holmes paused and suddenly said, 'Tell me, Mrs Hurst, do you think your butler plays the piano well?'

'My butler?' asked Mrs Hurst in some astonishment.

'Yes.'

'The one who brought the tea upstairs?'

'The very one.'

'But he does not play the piano, as far as I know.'

'Oh, pardon me, Mrs Hurst, but he does. The tips of his fingers are flat, which indicates that he must be a pianist.'

'It is strange that you should make that deduction, Mr Holmes, because there is no piano in the servants' quarters.'

'You have a piano. He might have used that.'

'I don't recall telling you I had a piano.'

'You didn't tell me. But you did mention that you caught him reading your sheet music. Where there is sheet music, there is a musical instrument. I naturally deduced a piano. They are all the rage at the moment in cultured homes like yours, Mrs Hurst. I also happened to notice a piano in one of your downstairs rooms when we arrived. Do you play?'

'I do not. My husband plays. He is quite accomplished.' Mrs Hurst paused for a moment, then changed her tone completely into a rather sharp one. 'Are you sure that my butler plays my piano?'

'I am convinced of it,' replied Holmes, in a voice that equalled Mrs Hurst's icy tone.

'Can you be sure?'

'I am sure. The seat of your butler's trousers was creased a great deal. The creasing continued for a small section of the upper part of his trouser leg. This would not occur in any chair, so he had to have sat on a stool for some period of time. I therefore deduced a piano stool. I think it best, Mrs Hurst, that you refrain from mentioning this to your butler. The slightest reference to it could jeopardize the entire plan that I have devised.'

'Very well, Mr Holmes. I shall not breathe a word about it.'

'In order to narrow our number of suspects down from almost the entire population of London cab drivers to less than a dozen, I shall have to ask you a few questions. Will you comply?'

'Most definitely, Mr Holmes. I am more than happy to do so.'

'Does your husband have any enemies at work?'

'No.'

'Do you have any enemies that you are aware of?'

'None that I am aware of.'

'Lastly, what were you wearing when you were in each of these cabs?'

'I wore a plain green dress, that I have had for many years, when I was in the first cab. In the second cab I was wearing a light blue dress beautifully made with a large bustle. In the third cab, I was wearing a brown silk outfit, the very latest design from Paris. I have not worn them since the incidents in question.'

'Capital. That was very wise of you. May I see them, please?' enquired Holmes.

'Why, certainly.' Mrs Hurst rose, left the room and returned presently with three fine dresses. Holmes began examining each one in turn.

A few minutes had elapsed when he remarked,'You were robbed in the same cab each time, Mrs Hurst.'

'How have you deduced that, Mr Holmes?' enquired Mrs Hurst, surprised at his certainty.

'My conclusion is based upon the fibres

that I found on the seat of each of your dresses. They are all the same, so you must have been in the same cab each time. These fibres are from the cushion you sat on in each cab. The design is quite unique. There is a criss-cross pattern made of a tweed material. Very rare indeed. Such upholstery was a feature of the cab factory of Park and Fortescue of Newington Butts and was last produced in 1872.'

'Amazing,' marvelled Mrs Hurst.

'I haven't finished yet,' grumbled Holmes. 'I can also see that this cab had no metal rims round the wheels to prevent their splintering. This is an obvious deduction, owing to the several minute splinters that I have found on each of these dresses of yours,' explained Holmes. 'In case I forget, Mrs Hurst, what was the number of this cab?'

'Number, Mr Holmes?'

'Yes, Mrs Hurst,' replied Holmes. 'The Hackney Carriage Act states that vehicles for hire must clearly display a registered number as a means of identification.'

'It did have a number, Mr Holmes, I

suppose, but I am quite shortsighted and could not see it. I was always in too much of a state of distress really after each robbery to try to observe the number of the cab.'

Holmes sighed deeply. 'It is a great pity,' he remarked, 'that you were unable to observe the registration number of the cab. If you had, the case would be as good as solved. There is nothing more for us to see, I presume, Mrs Hurst?'

Mrs Hurst shook her head.

'Very well, Mrs Hurst, my friend, Dr Watson, and myself shall now retire to Baker Street to review these events in more detail. Do not hesitate to contact me for reassurance or guidance,' remarked Holmes.

Mrs Hurst escorted us to the front door and we set out for Baker Street. Once we had settled down into easy chairs and Holmes had lit a cigarette, we began to remark upon the case at hand.

'I am beginning to suspect, Watson, that Mrs Hurst is not confiding the entire truth to us.'

'Why would she not do that? After all,

she does want her case solved, Holmes.'

'Quite, but I am not too far from believing that she is protecting someone. Who it is and why she is doing this, if, as you point out, she does want her case solved, will probably remain a mystery. At least for the present. I am unsure about the complete innocence of Mrs Hurst, and her butler. At present I am suspecting the latter.

'I suggest that we go back to Cadogan Place this evening, Watson, when we will be able to follow the butler should he leave the house once he is off duty. He may solve this mystery for us or he may not. We need to track him stealthily from a distance, Watson, in case we miss some vital clues.'

At about ten that evening we departed for Cadogan Place. When we arrived, Holmes insisted that our cab driver stop at the southern end of Cadogan Place, rather than outside number 51. Once we had paid our fare and dismounted, we found a place of concealment where we hid for half an hour before the butler finally appeared. He hailed a cab. We followed at a distance in another cab. We trundled over Chelsea Bridge, down Queenstown Road, then right into Battersea Park Road. Our pursuit continued through the vast complex of the intricately woven streets of Battersea till his journey ended in Devereux Road where he dismounted and entered number 21.

We waited in our cab. If our steed had not been so fidgety, we would not have had to wait so long to dismount. We were perfectly justified in being cautious. If we had not been so and the butler had realized he was being followed, that would have brought about the ruination of our whole campaign.

Once we were confident that our suspect had actually gone inside, and was not lurking in the shadows, we shared the cost of the journey between us. Holmes then implored our cab driver to depart as noiselessly as possible, so that the noise of the horse's hooves would not alert anyone in number 21 and cause a glance out of the window.

'I think our fish may be well and truly in the net,' whispered Holmes to me.

'What have you observed which makes you think so?' I enquired, as quietly as I possibly could, without being inaudible.

'Well, a hansom cab parked outside the house does give the game away somewhat.'

Holmes was perfectly correct, for outside number 21 was a hansom cab. We approached it steathily, uncertain if someone was inside or not. Once we had ascertained there was indeed no one inside, Holmes set to work. Naturally, we approached with the cab positioned between us and the house which the butler had entered. We took advantage of the cab's presence and used it as cover. Holmes worked quickly. It took him only a few minutes to discover the cab's identity, that this was indeed the cab that had transported Mrs Hurst to and from her house.

'See, Watson, there are no metal rims round the wheels to prevent splintering. Unless I am very much mistaken, this is the very weapon we are looking for.' Holmes eased himself up higher into the cab, then remarked, 'Yes, as I thought.

The fabric on the cushion is tweed and the pattern is criss-crossed. I suspected it would be so.'

He silently climbed down from the cab, clasped my arm with his customary iron grip, then pulled me towards him.

'Let us be gone, Watson. There is nothing more we can do here.'

We strode to the end of Devereux Road, and turned into Broomwood Road, where we hailed a cab and were soon bowling along through Battersea.

'Firstly, Watson, Baker Street, then on to Cadogan Place,' remarked Holmes.

'Why Baker Street first?'

'I have some explaining to do, Watson. No doubt many aspects of this case have bewildered you. I intend to make you feel less in the dark, not only for yourself, but should you wish to have this published, for your readers too.'

I thanked Holmes. Once we had arrived at Baker Street and made ourselves comfortable in Holmes's apartment, he began to explain the case in unparalleled detail. Before he began his explanation, he stuffed his pipe full of tobacco until almost overflowing. He lounged back in his armchair, puffing away for a few minutes, then he began.

'We are nearing the termination of this case, Watson. We have only a few loose ends left. Even though this case is almost solved, certain aspects of it still prove to be bewildering. For instance, Watson, does your maid go home on a Tuesday evening for a meal and return early Wednesday morning?'

'Why, no,' I replied. 'She takes a day off of her own choosing once a month at the weekend.'

'Quite, Watson. That is definitely the norm, although whether such a degree of lenience would prevail towards butlers, or this particular butler, is yet to be seen. I would expect Mrs Hurst's butler to visit and return home some time during the weekend. He, however, visits his family's residence in Battersea on a Tuesday, which is a most unusual and suspicious day.'

'How can it be suspicious?' I enquired, failing completely to grasp Holmes's meaning.

'For a butler not to visit his home during the weekend implies that there must be another day far more preferable to him. For him to be given 'home leave' on that day can mean only one of three things. Either he must have considerable influence over Mrs Hurst, possibly because she is in fear of him, which seems most unlikely. Or she is a particularly lax employer. Or he has a genuine reason, such as urgent family business, to take an unorthodox day off.'

'Is there not another possibility, Holmes?' I asked rather cautiously, in view of Holmes's occasionally violent temper.

'Perhaps you would care to enlighten me, Watson?' enquired Holmes, showing no sign of any ill will.

'No. I feel I have made a mistake in my recollection of this case to be able to find another reason,' I answered.

'Watson, I insist. This reason of yours, however trivial and worthless it may seem to you, may provide me with the vital link to complete my chain of reasoning. So, please, Watson, what is it?'

'Well, Holmes, there could be a

relationship between them which would explain why she was so very lenient towards him.'

'Watson!' bellowed Holmes at the top of his voice, making the windows rattle. 'That is the most absurd and ridiculous thing I have ever heard anyone say, least of all you! That is preposterous! A lady of Mrs Hurst's social standing having a relationship with a mere butler! Oh, honestly, Watson, I expected from you more sense than that! I am flabbergasted at you, Watson. How can you think of such a thing, let alone say it? Let us both be sure of one thing, Watson, that in British society, butlers do not have relationships with their mistress employers. Is that quite clear?'

I instantly nodded assent, for this harsh rebuttal had taken my breath away. I dared not speak, even murmur, for a lengthy period of time after Holmes's rudest and sharpest rebuke ever. I was increasingly regretting having made my stupid suggestion to Holmes. As each silent minute passed, I regretted it more and more.

The silence was broken by Holmes.

'Watson, should you ever make such a stupid and inconceivable suggestion like that again, then I am afraid that I shall be forced to discontinue our friendship.'

This naturally made me keep my foolish tongue in my cheek for the rest of the evening. If I was asked a question, I would reply in monosyllabic tones to prevent Holmes losing his temper at me again and also, which was of great concern to me, I did not wish to lose him as a friend.

During the course of the evening, Holmes smoked five pipes of tobacco and consumed five large glasses of whisky and soda. During his consumption of tobacco and alcohol, he explained that he was less inclined to suspect the butler than he had been at the outset of the case. Holmes had deduced earlier by discreet questioning in the servants' quarters that the butler had an elder brother who had a long facial birthmark. This elder brother was consequently moved up in status to our prime suspect.

Holmes believed that the game was

most certainly afoot and remarked, 'We have not yet set our snare for I feel that there will be little need of one. It will all be to no avail!'

I must confess that I gasped somewhat at Holmes's extreme pessimism. This case must be troubling him deeply for him to be pessimistic. He wrung his bony hands together and then murmured, 'I very much fear, Watson, that the mere four times I have been beaten is likely to increase to five after this case.'

'Oh, no!' I exclaimed. 'Don't be so pessimistic. The case is not over yet. You may still solve it.'

'Thank you, Watson. I now know for certain that you have faith in me.'

'You mean your brief bout of pessimism was a pretence, enabling you to discover my loyalty?' I enquired.

'I do. I have to know where I stand. And now,' began Holmes, leaping from his chair as though he had been stung, 'let us return yet again to Cadogan Place for I suspect that the butler will have returned early.'

'Why should he return early?' Glancing

at the clock on the mantelpiece, I exclaimed, 'Surely it is not that late?'

'It is not late, Watson, yet I suspect that the butler will return to Mrs Hurst within the next few minutes with a long story to tell. Come, Watson,' he urged. 'Cadogan Place with all speed.'

Presently our cab arrived at Cadogan Place. Holmes rang the bell fiercely and the door was suddenly opened by a red-faced, short, stout servant who, judging by her apparel, was the cook.

'Sir?' she asked, with a pronounced Cockney accent.

'Madam,' began Holmes, 'I understand that Mrs Hurst employs a butler here, who returned a few minutes ago.'

'That's right, sir. He's upstairs in the sitting room with Mrs Hurst. I'll show you the way, sir.'

We were ushered upstairs into the sitting room. Mrs Hurst was addressing the butler who was hanging his head in shame. Holmes dismissed the cook and we both crossed the room towards them.

'Mrs Hurst, is there something amiss?' questioned Holmes.

'That is what I am trying to find out,' she answered. Then, turning to the butler asked him, 'Why have you returned so early?'

Holmes interrupted before the butler could answer, 'Pray, sit down, Mrs Hurst. I shall explain for you.'

He then ordered the butler and myself to be seated, too.

'To begin with, Mrs Hurst, your butler is entirely innocent of any crime or injustice against you. He returned here on hearing some bad news of a family nature. This news was not of an impending funeral, it was of theft and unsavoury dealings. I am right, am I not?' asked Holmes, addressing the butler.

'You are entirely correct, sir,' he replied.

'When you returned home today, it was because you suspected the injustices inflicted on Mrs Hurst were committed by your brother. I am fully aware of the events that followed this, so continue the series of events for Mrs Hurst.'

'Very well, sir. On hearing of the actions my brother had taken in obtaining cash for his own advancement, I was deeply shocked and ashamed of being his younger brother. I ordered him to return the money to Mrs Hurst and he refused to do so. I told him that I was so disgusted by his behaviour that I wished never to be acquainted with him again. I stormed out of the house in a rage and came straight here. I realized after your visit here, Mr Holmes, that my brother acquired his cash by charging Mrs Hurst extortionate sums for travelling trivial distances in the cab he had borrowed from our father.'

Mrs Hurst gasped upon hearing this.

'How was your brother able to borrow a cab from your father?' enquired Holmes.

'My father owns a little run-down cab firm with only two cabs and almost no money for investment. It is in a most under-financed state.'

'I can well believe that,' interrupted Holmes. 'So this declining business had a cab to spare?'

'Yes.'

'Was this cab used occasionally?'

'Yes, by my brother.'

'So, you are telling us that your brother stole from Mrs Hurst using the other cab from your father's business. This business must be extremely run down for it to have not even enough space for you to keep the second cab under cover.'

'That is so. That is why the second cab is parked outside my father's house.'

'What does your brother intend to do with the money he stole?' I enquired.

'He intends to use the money to start a new life in France.'

'Where is he at present?' asked Holmes.

'On his way to Dover by now, I assume.'

'Do you wish us to pursue him?' Holmes instantly asked Mrs Hurst.

'There is no need,' the butler interjected. 'Before I left my father's house, I went to my brother's room and took the liberty of removing this bag of money,' he remarked, holding it up in his right hand. 'It felt suspiciously heavy, so I assumed it was what he had stolen from Mrs Hurst. That is why I brought it here. It contains the sum of fifteen guineas.'

'The very sum of which I was robbed!' exclaimed Mrs Hurst, taking the bag from the butler's outstretched hand.

Mrs Hurst thanked us heartily for our services and escorted us to the front door and we were soon comfortably back in Baker Street.

'Holmes, have you deduced why the butler played Mrs Hurst's piano?'

'I have indeed,' chuckled Holmes. 'One of Mr Hurst's birthday cards on the mantelpiece of the sitting room explained the whole affair. The butler had been practising on the piano solely in order to play Mr Hurst's favourite piece of music to him on his birthday. Mrs Hurst had arranged it all with the butler. And now, Watson. A cigarette?'

THE END